Jane Eyre

Adapted by Mary Sebag-Montefiore

from the story by
Charlotte Brontë

Reading consultant: Alison Kelly
Edited by Jane Chisholm and Rachel Firth
Designed by Sarah Cronin
Illustrated by Elena Selivanova

First published in 2017 by Usborne Publishing Ltd., Usborne House,
83-85 Saffron Hill, London EC1N 8RT, England.
www.usborne.com

A CIP catalogue record for this book is available from the British Library.

Contents

Chapter 1

The Red Room

There was no possibility of taking a walk that day. The cold winter wind had brought with it dark clouds and cruel rain.

I was glad. I hated long walks on icy afternoons. Dreadful to me was the freezing cold nipping my fingers and toes, listening to Bessie, the nurse, telling me that my cousins, Eliza, John and Georgiana Reed, were better than me in every way.

Now Eliza, John and Georgiana snuggled up next to their mother, my Aunt Reed, on the drawing room sofa in front of the fire.

Next to the drawing room was a small study. I slipped inside, and taking the book I loved most from the bookcase – *Bewick's History of British Birds* – I climbed onto the window seat. There I sat, pulling the curtain shut, so that I was hidden.

I loved this book. Every picture told me a story, lifting me into other worlds. In my imagination, I flew along the white shores of the frozen north. I sailed on ships in calm seas, and I was happy at last.

The study door opened, and I heard John's voice.

"Jane? Bad animal, where are you?"

John was too dim to think of looking for me in an empty room, but Eliza poked her head around the door, announcing, "She'll be in the window seat."

I couldn't bear the thought of him dragging me out, so straightaway I came out of my own accord.

"What do you want?" I asked.

"Say, 'What do you want, MASTER REED?'" he replied. "I want you to come here."

John was fourteen, fat and pimpled. He bullied me, not once a day, but all the time, and no one spoke up for me. Aunt Reed worshipped her boy, and the servants were blind and deaf, not wanting to upset her, or their young master.

Without warning, he hit me in the face.

"That's for sneaking behind the curtain, and for that look in your eyes. What were you doing?"

"Reading."

"Show the book."

I put it into his hands.

"You have no right to take this book. It's mine. Gateshead Hall is mine, and so is everything in it. Mama says you're no better than a beggar. We're gentleman's children, and you're – dirt. Now, go and stand by the door."

I obeyed. I didn't know what he was going to do. Then I saw him lift the book, and hurl it at me. I ducked, but it hit me, and I fell. As blood trickled down my neck, I was filled, not with my usual terror, but, for the first time, with pure rage.

"Wicked, cruel boy,! I stormed. "You're like a murderer, like the Roman emperors!"

"Don't speak to me like that!" he yelled, grabbing me. I fought back. I don't know what my hands did, but I heard him squeal, "Rat! Rat!"

Eliza and Georgiana, Aunt Reed and Bessie came running to the study, and pulled us apart. John put his fists in his eyes, and cried loudly.

"Take her to the red room, and lock her in," ordered Mrs. Reed, giving me a withering glance.

They pulled me upstairs. With every step, I struggled. I usually gave in, but this time I knew I'd crossed a boundary, which made me feel stronger. I burned with passion against injustice.

Bessie pushed me onto a stool.

"Such a fury to fly at Master John," she scolded, taking off the garter holding up her stocking. "If you don't sit still, you must be tied down."

"Don't do that!" I cried. "I won't move."

"Mind you don't," said Bessie. "You should be grateful to Mrs. Reed. She could easily turn you out of here. You have nothing. You have to remember that. You should be humble and try to make yourself agreeable."

She left me alone, locking the door behind her.

The red room was never used. It was cold, solemn and dark, with deep red curtains shrouding the windows, and a huge bed with massive mahogany pillars. It was here that Mr. Reed had died nine years ago. From this bed, he had been lifted and laid in his coffin. His portrait hung here, above a chest where Mrs. Reed locked her jewels.

I sat on the stool, watching the light fading as rain beat on the windows. With every hour that passed, my anger grew.

"NOT FAIR!" screamed the words in my head.

Why didn't they like me? Why did they treat me so badly? Eliza was bad-tempered and selfish, but no one corrected her. Georgiana, spoiled and rude, was pampered. John was never punished. Even when he twisted the necks of pigeons and killed baby chickens, he was his mother's darling.

If Mr. Reed had lived, he would surely have been kind to me. Did his spirit know how his sister's child was treated, I wondered? Perhaps it might leave the world of the dead and come to me.

Instantly, I was afraid. I leaped up. Out of the window, I glimpsed a moving light. Moonlight? No. The moon was still, but this light hovered, as if a phantom walked. It was probably a gleam from a lantern, but in my panic I knew it was a ghost.

I screamed. Then louder, again and again. Steps came running along the passage…it was Bessie.

"What's the matter?"

"Oh! I saw a light! A ghost! Let me out, please!"

Now I heard Aunt Reed coming, her silk dress rustling stormily.

"Let go of Bessie's hand. You won't leave the room with tricks like these."

"Oh, Aunt, please! Have pity! Punish me some other way!"

"Quiet. This violence is repulsive." She didn't believe my wild sobs, my terror. I heard the key turn in the lock. Fear and darkness swept over me, and with a final choking scream, I knew no more.

Chapter 2

Goodbye to Gateshead Hall

When I woke, I was in my own bed. Bessie leaned over me, a glass of milk in her hands.

"Would you like a drink, Jane?" she asked softly.

"No thank you."

So gentle was Bessie that I dared to ask her, "What is the matter with me?"

"You fell sick in the red room, with crying."

"That poor child," I heard her mutter to herself. "I wonder what she saw. Missis was too hard…"

I couldn't sleep. I was gripped by a dread that only children know. Yes, Mrs. Reed, I'll never forget that night. I ought to forgive you, but the memory of the red room has stayed with me forever.

Next day, I got up. Bessie brought me cake on a plate with a bird of paradise painted on it. I loved this plate, but I'd never been allowed to touch it. It was wasted now. I couldn't eat, and the bird meant nothing to me.

"Don't cry, Jane," said Bessie, but she might as well have said to the fire, "Don't burn."

Later, Mr. Lloyd came. He was not the doctor Mrs. Reed called upon for herself and her children, but a less important one she had for the servants.

"Up already?" asked Mr. Lloyd. "You're better, then. Can you tell me what made you ill?"

"I was shut up in a room where there's a ghost," I replied. "It was cruel to do that to me. I was afraid."

"Are you still afraid?"

"N-no. Just unhappy."

"Why?"

"I have no father or mother..." I began.

"But you have a kind aunt, and cousins. Don't you think you're lucky to live at Gateshead Hall?"

"But they say I have no right to live here."

"You don't want to leave it, surely?"

I thought about it. At the same time, Mr. Lloyd was asking, "Would you like to go to school?"

School! Yes, if it meant escaping from my aunt.

I nodded.

"Well, well. I'll see what I can do. I shall talk to Mrs. Reed when she returns."

For the next few days, I stayed in my room, but John kept darting in to find me. He jeered at me, and I looked the other way, but when he hit me, I hit him back. He ran blubbing to his mama.

"I told you not to go near her, John," I heard her say. "She's not fit to associate with you."

At that, I leaned over the bannisters and cried, "They are not fit to associate with *me*. You wouldn't dare if Uncle Reed were still alive. In heaven he can see all you do, and so can my parents. They know you hate me and want me dead!"

Mrs. Reed was big and plump, but on hearing this, she ran nimbly up the stairs and shook me.

"You wicked child," she hissed.

I half-thought she was right, for inside I felt only bad feelings. Christmas came and went, but I had no presents and stayed in my room. I saw Eliza and Georgiana run downstairs in party dresses with scarlet sashes, their hair elaborately curled in ringlets. I heard the piano, the hum of conversation, and the jingling of glass and china. If it hadn't been for Bessie, I don't know how I'd have managed.

After weeks of loneliness, Bessie told me Mrs. Reed wanted to see me.

It was so long since I'd been downstairs, I felt afraid. Opening the door, I saw a black pillar, with a grim face. At least, that's how it seemed.

"This is the little girl I spoke of," Aunt Reed said. "Her mother was my dead husband's sister. She's no relation of mine. She has no claim on me."

He, for the pillar was a man, turned his head. "She is small. How old is she?"

"Ten."

"So much?" He considered me. "Your name?"

"Jane Eyre, sir."

"Well, Jane Eyre, are you a good child?"

"Perhaps the less said about that, the better, Mr. Brocklehurst," said Mrs. Reed.

"So you are bad," he informed me. "Do you know where the wicked go after they are dead?"

"They go to hell," I replied.

"What is hell, little girl?"

"A pit full of fire."

"Would you like to fall into that pit and burn there forever?"

"No, sir."

"Then how may you avoid it?" he asked.

I thought about it.

"I must keep well and not die."

"What a reply! That proves you have a wicked heart. You must pray to God to change it," he said.

Mrs. Reed interrupted with a smile I didn't like.

"Mr. Brocklehurst, I should like Jane to go to

your school, Lowood. She will remain at school in the holidays. I warn you, you must keep a strict eye on her. She tells lies. She is deceitful."

I trembled with injustice. How could I be free to be myself at this new school, if they knew before I got there that I was bad? She'd taken away all hope for my new life.

But Mr. Brocklehurst was nodding in agreement.

Before he left, Mr. Brocklehurst gave me a book.

"Read this story, Jane Eyre, about a naughty child like you, a liar, and her sudden death. Think what happened to her. Think of the fires of hell."

"Go to your room, Jane," said Mrs. Reed.

No. Speak, I must.

"I am not deceitful. I don't tell lies. Give this book to your children. They lie..."

She glared at me, but I went on —

"If anyone asks me how you treated me, I'll say you treated me with cruelty."

"How dare you!" she exploded.

"How dare I? Because it is the truth. You think

that I can do without one bit of love or kindness, but I can't. You have no pity. I'll never forget how you pushed me back into the red room, when I begged for mercy. People think you are a good woman, but you're bad. You are deceitful."

I felt as though a tight band had burst open, making me free. I watched Mrs. Reed get up and leave the room. I'd made her go! Yes, I was the winner. Revenge was sweet.

But my triumph collapsed. Guilt overwhelmed me. I didn't like the feelings of hate inside me. I was ready to apologize, but I knew that Mrs. Reed would have scorned and rejected me.

I went to Bessie.

"I'm going to school," I told her.

"Won't you be sorry to leave?"

"Not I!"

"You are put upon, that's for certain."

She gave me a hug, and that night she told me stories until I went to sleep. Even for me, life had its gleams of sunshine.

Chapter 3

School

A few days later, I left. A coach was to pick me up at 6 a.m. I was ready to go by 5. Bessie was the only one to see me off, with her lantern light shining on the frosted steps of Gateshead Hall.

I heard the distant roll of wheels announcing the coach's arrival. Its four horses pulled to a halt, snorting in the icy air. The passengers inside stared at me with curiosity.

"Is she going by herself?" asked the coachman.

I clung to Bessie, kissing her.

"Yes, she's all alone. Take care of her," said

Bessie, hugging me back. Then the door slammed shut and we drove off.

I don't remember much of the journey, just the mist turning darker as morning melted into afternoon and then to dusk. I heard a wild wind rushing among trees and at last, I slept.

When I woke, I was being lifted, and set down on a wet, pebbly path. Rain and darkness filled the air. A lady, waiting for me with an umbrella, led me towards lighted windows at the end of the path.

"I am Miss Temple. And you are Jane Eyre? Is this the first time you've left your parents?"

"My parents are dead."

She took me into a long room lit by candles, full of girls sitting at tables, studying. They wore thin frocks and pinafores, their hair pulled back tightly.

"Monitors, bring the trays!" Miss Temple called.

Four girls came in holding trays on each of which was a pitcher of water and a mug. I drank thirstily, but I was too tired and too excited to eat. I saw what supper consisted of, though. Thin oat biscuits, broken into pieces.

At bedtime, I was taken to a dormitory, lined with long rows of beds. We undressed in silence. The single candle was blown out, and I fell asleep.

I was woken by a bell. It wasn't yet light. I crept out of bed reluctantly. I was shivering with cold and there was only one basin for every six girls – and the water was frozen. Then a bell rang again and, two by two, we marched downstairs to a cold, dark schoolroom. For a whole hour, we listened to Bible chapters read aloud until the bell rang again. A long grace was said, followed by hymns, and finally the meal began. I plunged my spoon into my bowl.

Burned porridge.

"Not again," several girls muttered.

It made me feel sick. I couldn't eat it. I saw each girl try to swallow it, and then lay down her spoon.

We said another grace in thanks for what we had not received, and then lessons began. These lasted for three hours. I felt totally strange in this new world, and cold and hungry. I was shocked, too, when the teacher, Miss Scatcherd, kept picking on one girl all the time, for nothing, it seemed to me.

"Helen Burns, hold up your head. Helen Burns, you dirty, disagreeable girl, your nails are filthy. Have you not washed this morning?"

Why doesn't Helen explain that she couldn't wash because the water was frozen? I wondered.

"Fetch the rod," Miss Scatcherd ordered, and when Helen obeyed, Miss Scatcherd beat her neck with sharp, hard strokes. I quivered with anger, but Helen's calm, sweet expression didn't change.

"Disobedient girl," screeched Miss Scatcherd.

Seeing the trace of a tear on Helen's cheek, at playtime, I went up to her. She was alone, reading.

"How could you bear it when Miss Scatcherd whipped you? She's cruel..."

Not really. I know I annoy her. I do have faults. I'm careless. I forget rules. I should try to do better."

"I couldn't bear it," I stated.

"Yes you could," Helen replied gently. "It's weak and silly to say you can't do things, when you must."

"But I hate anyone who treats me wrongly."

"The Bible says we should love our enemies, and be good to those who hate us."

"Then I should love Mrs. Reed, and John!" I told her all about them. "Well?" I asked her impatiently. "Don't you think Mrs. Reed is a hard, bad woman?"

"Yes," Helen admitted. "But life is too short to hold a grudge. You'd be happier, Jane, if you let it go and try to forgive."

One day, the whole school was summoned as Mr. Brocklehurst strode in with his wife, and other ladies, all dressed warmly in velvet and furs. We shivered in our thin frocks while he inspected us.

"Who is that girl with red curls?" he demanded.

"Julia Severn, sir," replied Miss Temple.

"Her hair is an abomination. Cut it off, close to her head. Modesty and plainness is what these girls must strive for. In fact," he thundered, "ALL girls with long hair or curls must have it cut off."

"I see you noted a complaint about burned porridge. Do you not REALIZE that these children must learn to endure any little disappointment? I am helping them to God."

I shrank into my chair. A fatal move.

"Who is that girl who moved?"

"Jane Eyre, sir."

"Jane Eyre, is it? Ah. Stand upon this stool, Jane Eyre. Here. Where everyone can see you."

"Ladies, teachers, children, see this girl. She looks just like other children, but she is a liar. Keep away from her. Her good aunt had to send her away, to prevent her own children from being infected."

"Shocking! Dreadful!" I heard his ladies mutter.

"She will stand on this stool all morning. No one is to speak to her all day," he finished.

There I stood, alone, as the whole school stared.

I saw Helen smile at me. That smile warmed me and inspired me. As soon as Mr Brocklehurst left, she took me to Miss Temple's room. She was coughing, and for a moment I forgot my own sorrows to be vaguely anxious about her.

"I can't bear to think that everyone will despise

me," I cried. "If I'm not loved, I'd rather die."

"Be strong, Jane," she said, knocking at Miss Temple's door.

"I'm glad Helen brought you here," said Miss Temple, putting her arms around me. "Have you cried your grief away? I don't believe what Mr. Brocklehurst said," she went on. "I know you're a good girl. Go on as you have begun, and you will see no one will take any notice of him. How is your cough, Helen? Does your chest still hurt?"

"I'm a little better," said Helen.

Miss Temple took her hand, felt her pulse, and gave a little sigh. She stoked up the fire, put the kettle to boil, and set a tray upon a little table, laid with a bright teapot, china, and a plate of cake that she took out of a cupboard. "My own supply," she said. We sat one each side of her by the fire, talking. I basked in the warmth, and her kindness. A sense of peace crept over me and I relaxed. I decided I must make a success of Lowood, for Miss Temple's sake and for Helen's.

Chapter 4

Goodbye, Helen

The icy weather turned into spring, but with the sunshine came – disease. Typhus fever felled us like a tide, fed by our semi-starvation, the unclean water we drank and the foul earth of bogs and pestilence on which Lowood was built. Some pupils died, some went home to die. Helen was in bed, ill. She had no home to go to. She, like me, was an orphan.

Every day I asked a teacher, "Can I see Helen Burns?"

"Certainly not. She's far too ill."

One night, I couldn't bear it any more. I must see Helen. I heard she'd been taken into Miss Temple's room. There I crept, and I saw her, in a little bed, next to Miss Temple's.

"Helen," I whispered. "Are you awake?"

"Jane?" she asked in her own gentle voice. "Why are you here? It's past 11 o'clock."

"Oh! She sounds like herself. Perhaps she's getting better," I thought.

But a terrible fit of coughing silenced her. Later, when she could get her breath, she whispered, "Have you come to say goodbye?"

Her meaning dawned on me, and I cried, "Don't die, Helen, please don't!"

"I'm happy," she said, with her sweet smile. "Look, your feet are bare. You're shivering. Come and cover yourself with my quilt."

"But where will you go when you die? What is death?" I sobbed.

"I believe I will go to God."

"What is God?"

"I think I'll find out. I believe it's a place of happiness."

I flung my arms around her, as she murmured, "Don't leave me, Jane. I like you being near."

"I'll stay," I promised, nestling next to her. "No one shall take me away. Dear Helen."

"Goodnight, Jane."

"Goodnight, Helen."

She kissed me, and I kissed her, and soon we both slept. When I woke, I was in my own bed. Miss Temple had carried me there, she told me later. She'd gone to Helen and discovered us, our arms around each other. I was asleep, and Helen was… dead.

Chapter 5

The Rider in the Moonlight

So many children died at Lowood that everyone talked about the terrible conditions. After that, things improved. We moved to another building, we had better food and warmer clothes.

I stayed there for eight more years, six as pupil, two as teacher. Then, I began to feel restless. I wanted new faces, new places... I decided to advertise for a post as a governess.

It was answered by a Mrs. Fairfax of Thornfield Hall, seventy miles away, who needed a governess for a little girl, Adèle.

Just before I left Lowood, Bessie came to see me.

"I heard you were going away, and I wanted to see you. My, you've grown into a young lady. Not a beauty, but you were never pretty as a child."

"How are they all at Gateshead?" I asked.

Missis has got very stout, and is always worrying about Master John, because he spends such a lot of money, and Miss Eliza and Miss Georgiana are always quarrelling. I'm married now, and I've got a baby girl who I've named Jane. A relative of yours came to Gateshead, a Mr. Eyre, your father's brother, but Missis said you were at school fifty miles off. He went away, very disappointed, to Madeira. Missis was very impatient with him."

I was surprised to hear I had an uncle, but there was no way I could contact him.

I prepared for my journey to my new home, trying to make myself neat and tidy. I turned away from the mirror sadly. Why had nature made me small, pale, with irregular features?

I arrived at Thornfield Hall so late that I couldn't

see the house properly. An elderly lady sat knitting by the fire. She looked the picture of domesticity, not stately, not grand, and my shyness fled.

"Mrs. Fairfax?" I asked.

"Yes, do sit down, and Leah shall bring you a hot drink and sandwiches."

I was surprised to be treated like a visitor.

"Shall I see Miss Fairfax tonight?" I asked.

"Miss Fairfax? Oh, you mean Miss Varens. She is Mr. Rochester's ward."

"Who is Mr. Rochester?"

She looked surprised. "The owner of Thornfield."

"But I thought you..." I faltered.

"Bless you, no, what an idea! I'm the housekeeper. To be sure, Mr. Rochester is a distant cousin, but I never presume on the relationship. It'll be nice to have some company. There's no one here except for servants, Leah, and John and his wife. And little Adèle and her nurse, of course."

Later, she took me to my room, up a staircase, along a vaulted gallery which looked more like a church than a house, so great was the space and chill. My bedroom, thankfully, was small and cheerful, very different from the bare planks of Lowood. I felt I'd be happy here, and lay down full of hope.

When I woke, I dressed quickly and went outside to see the house properly. It was three stories high, with battlements at the top, where rooks flew in and out. Surrounding the house were gnarled thorn trees, and further off were hills, which seemed to embrace Thornfield in its own loneliness.

As I was thinking this, I saw Mrs. Fairfax with a little girl, aged about seven, with curls down to her waist, who ran towards me.

"C'est là ma gouvernante?" she asked.

"She's French?" I asked, shocked.

"She is. I can't understand her. Do you think you will be able to?"

Luckily, I'd learned French from a Frenchwoman at Lowood, and was fluent enough. Adèle chattered away. She found it hard to concentrate. I could see she'd never had to before. After lunch I thought she'd had enough and sent her back to her nurse.

Mrs. Fairfax showed me over the house. Huge rooms, darkened by imperfect light struggling through narrow windows, were filled with carved furniture that looked a hundred years old. It seemed like a shrine to memory, a place of stillness. We climbed the stairs, up to the third floor.

"See the view from here," said Mrs. Fairfax, and I looked out over a flat roof where the rooks flew, onto gardens, woods, hills and sky. We walked down a long corridor with doors on each side, all shut.

The last sound I expected to hear struck my ear. A laugh. A low sound, rising to an unearthly peal.

"What was that?" I asked.

"Grace Poole," said Mrs. Fairfax. "She sews in one of these rooms. Sometimes Leah is with her, and they're often noisy. GRACE!" she demanded.

I didn't expect any Grace to answer: that laugh was inhuman. But the door opened and a woman with a hard, plain face came out. Anyone less likely to make such a sound could scarcely be imagined.

"Not so much noise, Grace," ordered Mrs. Fairfax, and Grace curtsied, and went back in.

Three months passed. In that time I grew fond of Adèle. She wasn't clever, but she was loving. Mrs. Fairfax was kind, and I knew I was lucky to be here. But I still felt restless. I wasn't discontented. It was my nature to want my mind to have more to stimulate it.

One day, when Adèle had a cold and I'd settled her by the fire, I went for a walk. On this still winter afternoon, the moon rose, pale as a cloud. Silence surrounded me. The only sound was the tinkling of the little brook. I sat on a stile to drink in the solitude, watching the mist rising in ribbons.

I heard a clatter... a horse was coming. Out of the gloom, a huge dog emerged, followed by the horse, and on its back, a cloaked rider, like figures in a dream. There was a sliding sound, a fall.

"What the deuce to do now?" the man cried,

as he struggled to be free of his horse's reins.

In the bright moonlight, I saw a dark face with stern features and angry eyes. He wasn't handsome, or I should have felt shy.

"I live just below," I said. "I can get help."

"You live down there?"

"At Thornfield Hall," I said.

"Who are you?" he demanded

"I am the governess."

"Ah, the governess. I had forgotten." He tried to rise, wincing in pain. "Can you get hold of my horse's bridle and lead him to me?"

Normally I'd have been too frightened to touch such a snorting beast. I tried to obey, but it refused to let me near it. After watching my futile attempts to avoid its trampling forefeet, the man laughed.

"Come here," he said. "Excuse me. Necessity compels me to make you useful."

Leaning his heavy hand on my shoulder, he limped to his horse, and sprang into the saddle, grimacing grimly, for doing so wrenched his sprain.

"Thank you," he said, and then he cantered away. The dog rushed in his traces, and all three vanished.

Returning home, I listened for horse's hooves, and searched for a rider in a cloak with a dog, but I heard only the faintest waft of wind and saw only the moonbeams. I didn't like going back into Thornfield. Mrs. Fairfax with her knitting, my lonely little room, a quiet evening, night after night... was this my life?

But in the hall, the fire blazed, and in front of it lay the dog I'd seen earlier.

"Whose dog is this?" I asked Leah.

"That's Pilot. He's Mr. Rochester's dog. Mr. Rochester has just arrived. His horse slipped on the ice, and he's sprained his ankle. Mrs. Fairfax and Miss Adèle are with him."

Adèle was not easy to teach the next day. She kept staring at the wild, snowy garden, wondering if Mr. Rochester had brought her a present, till dusk, when Mrs. Fairfax came with a message.

"Mr. Rochester wants you and Adèle to take tea

with him in the drawing room."

In the drawing room, with Mrs. Fairfax, was my traveller of yesterday. I knew him by his grim mouth and jaw, his black hair, his jet eyebrows. The dog, Pilot, lay by the fire, and Adèle knelt by him, stroking him.

"Mon cadeau," she pleaded. "And for Miss Eyre?"

"Sit down, Miss Eyre, he said, not taking his eyes from the dog and the child, sounding impatient and formal at the same time, as though he was actually saying, "What does it matter to me whether Miss Eyre is there or not?"

I was not embarrassed. Politeness would have confused me more. I was interested to see how he would go on.

"Cadeau?" he said gruffly. "Did you expect a present, Miss Eyre? Are you fond of them?"

"I have little experience of them, sir."

"You are not like Adèle who demands one the minute she sees me. I find her much improved. You have taken trouble with her."

"Thank you, sir."

"You have been in my house for three months?"

"Yes, sir."

"And you came from — ?"

"Lowood school, sir. I was there for eight years."

"I know it. A charity school. Eight years? No wonder you have a look on your face as if you came from another world. When I saw you last night, I wondered if you'd bewitched my horse. I'm still not sure. How old are you?"

"Eighteen, sir."

"Do you have any family?"

"No, sir. I am an orphan."

"Who recommended you to come here?"

"I advertised, and Mrs. Fairfax answered."

"I'm glad for the good luck that brought her here," said Mrs. Fairfax. "She's been a companion to me, and a kind teacher to Adèle."

"I'll judge for myself," replied Mr. Rochester. "After all, she began by felling my horse."

Mrs. Fairfax looked bewildered, but Mr.

Rochester went on, "Mr. Brocklehurst was the director, wasn't he? No doubt you worshipped him."

"Oh no."

"You sound icy, Miss Eyre. I am surprised."

"I disliked Mr. Brocklehurst, and I was not alone. He's a harsh man. He starved us, bored us with long lectures, and read to us about sudden deaths and judgements which made us afraid to go to bed."

"What did you learn at Lowood? The piano?"

"A little."

"Of course. Everybody says that. Play now."

I did so, till he called out, "Stop! You play a little. Better than some but not well. Adèle showed me your sketchbook earlier. Are the drawings your work, or did somebody help you?"

"I did them myself," I said quickly.

"Ah, your pride is hurt." He picked up my sketchbook and began to turn its pages. He examined first my picture of clouds over a raging sea, with a cormorant holding a gold bracelet in its beak. The second was a dark twilight sky in which you could just see a woman's shape, in shades as soft as I could make them. The third was of an iceberg piercing the northern lights in a ring of white flame, against a background of black drapery."

"You painted these out of your own head?"

"I did, sir."

"Have you other imaginings of the same kind within?"

"Better, I hope, sir."

"Were you happy when you painted them?"

"I was... yes, happier than I've ever been."

"That's not saying much. Your pleasures have been few. It's nine o'clock. You've let Adèle stay up too late. Put her to bed."

Abruptly, he left the room.

"He's very changeable..." I said to Mrs. Fairfax.

"It's true. He's had family problems..."

"But he has no family."

"He's had much to make him shun this house..."

It was clear she wished to drop the subject, and accordingly, I did so.

Chapter 6

Evil Midnight Laughter

Over the next few days, I saw little of Mr. Rochester. Then Leah told me he wanted me to bring Adèle to him. On the table by him was a large box. Adèle recognized it instantly.

"Mon cadeau!"

She ripped it open. Out tumbled a rose-hued dress, a wreath of rosebuds and white satin slippers.

"Ah!" she gasped.

"Yes, run away and put it on," said Mr. Rochester. Then he turned to me. "You puzzle me, Miss Eyre. Tell me about yourself."

I was silent. I couldn't speak for the sake of it.

"Did I sound arrogant?" he asked. "I'm sorry."

I must have smiled, because he said, "I'm glad to see you smile, but speak too."

"I was thinking that very few masters would mind that their servants were hurt by their orders."

"Ah. I pay you. I'd forgotten. Not one in three thousand governesses would have answered as you have done. You speak your mind, and hide your faults well."

I raised my eyebrows; he read my glance.

"You are right," he continued. "*I* have plenty of faults. I have led an… interesting life, which many would sneer at. I've gone wrong. Goodness knows I wish I had my past again. I wish I'd stood firm."

I felt bold enough to voice my thoughts. "You could repent, sir, and try again?"

"Repentance is useless. Though I'm cursed, I will be happy, cost me what it may. I'll grasp at pleasure, like the honey the bee gathers on the moor."

"It may sting, taste bitter, sir."

"How do you know? Are you afraid of me, Miss Eyre, when I talk like a sphinx?"

"Not afraid, sir. Bewildered. I don't understand you. You say you are not as good as you'd like to be, but it seems to me that it's possible to become as one would wish to be, if one tries hard enough."

"Rightly said, Miss Eyre. I think I see between the bars of the cage that Lowood made a restless captive. If it were free, it would soar sky high. Am I right? One day you will be natural with me, because I find I cannot be conventional with you. Then you will have more spirit than you dare give me now."

I hesitated. "It's late. I must put Adèle to bed."

"Wait. She'll be down in a moment in her new dress. Did you wonder if she was my secret daughter? Well, she's not. I knew her mother in Paris. A beautiful woman. Did I love her? Yes, but she ran away with a musician and abandoned her child. I wanted to give Adèle a chance. Does the child's background shock you?"

"No, sir. I'd rather look after a waif like

Adèle than a spoiled brat."

As I spoke, Adèle danced in, twirling her dress. "Merci, Monsieur! It's beautiful!"

"You see, Miss Eyre, my intentions are good."

As the weeks passed, we talked more, every evening. He always had a smile for me. He was my friend, not my master: gentle, kind, warmer than the brightest fire, though to others I saw he was moody, proud, severe. I knew he was unhappy, and wished I could help him.

Mrs. Fairfax had told me he seldom stayed at Thornfield for more than a fortnight. I dreaded his going. This was my thought one night as I blew out my candle and lay down in my bed. I couldn't sleep. Downstairs, the clock struck two. I thought I heard murmurs... I heard fingers pass my bedroom door, as though they were groping their way down the gallery outside.

"Who's there?" I cried, chilled with fear.

No answer. Only a low, demonic laugh. The same that I had heard once before. This time it came from the very keyhole of my door, followed by a moan. Then I smelled burning. Trembling, I opened my door. The air was dim with smoke. Mr. Rochester's door was open, and I could see darting tongues of flame. I rushed inside. The curtains to his bed were on fire, but even in the midst of the blaze, he lay in deep sleep. I saw a water jug and basin, both full, and I flung them in his face.

"Jane? What have you done?" he exclaimed. "Are you a witch? Are you drowning me?"

"No, sir, but there's been a fire."

He lit his candle and looked at his bed, all blackened and scorched, the sheets drenched.

"Wait here, Jane, be still as a mouse till I return. I must visit the third floor. Just be still. If you're cold, put on my cloak. Don't move. Don't call anyone."

I watched till the light of his candle vanished. I was left in total darkness. A long time passed.

When he came back, he was pale and depressed.

"It is as I thought," he said. "I forgot to ask if you heard anything when you opened your door?"

"Yes. Grace Poole, a servant who sews here, she was laughing."

"Just so. Grace Poole. Don't say anything about this, Jane. I shall account for it in my own way."

"Goodnight, then, sir," I said.

"What!" he exclaimed. "Going already? You saved my life! Snatched me from a cruel and horrible death! At least shake hands."

Clasping my hand, he said, "I knew you would do me good, Jane. I saw it in your eyes when I first saw you. My good genie… my cherished preserver."

There was a strange energy in his voice, a strange fire in his look.

"I'm glad I was awake," I said, and then turned away. I went back to bed.

I couldn't sleep. My thoughts disturbed me till morning came. In the hours of night, I swam in an unquiet sea where waves of trouble rolled beneath surges of joy. I thought I saw beyond the wild waters a sweet, calm shore, but I couldn't get to it. A breeze on the water always took me away.

Chapter 7

Mystery... Misery

After a sleepless night, I wanted to see Mr. Rochester. I had so many questions. I needed answers.

He wasn't there. I did see Grace Poole in his bedroom, sewing rings on his new bed curtains, intent on her work. She had no sign of desperation about her, not as one would expect of a would-be murderess.

"Good morning, miss," she said, in her usual, matter-of-fact voice as she sewed on another ring.

I'll question her, I thought. "Good morning,

Grace. These are new bed curtains?"

"Master fell asleep with the candle lit last night, and the curtains caught fire, but luckily he woke and put it out with the water jug."

"Strange," I said. "No one heard?"

Now I detected a wariness in her.

"The servants sleep so far off, miss. Mrs. Fairfax is near, but she's old and the old sleep so heavy. But you are young. Did you hear a noise?"

"I did. At first I thought it was Mr. Rochester's dog, but a dog cannot laugh. I'm certain I heard a laugh, and a strange one."

"It's hardly likely master would laugh when he was in danger. You must have been dreaming."

"I was not."

"Have you told master you heard a laugh?"

"I have not seen him this morning."

"Did you see anything last night, miss?"

She's cross-questioning me, I thought. I must be on guard.

"On the contrary, Grace. I locked my door."

"Do you always do so?"

She wants to know my habits, I realized. Be careful…

"In future, I will," I said.

"That would be wise," said Grace, threading her needle.

All day, my thoughts troubled me. Who was Grace Poole? What was her history? Why had Mr. Rochester sworn me to secrecy? Mr. Rochester…

Ah, said the secret voice that speaks in our hearts. You are not beautiful, but you've felt Mr. Rochester likes you. His voice, his words, his look…

I was longing to see him again.

The day passed. I waited. Surely there would be a message for me to join him… all day I kept imagining I heard his tread. I constantly turned to the door, expecting him. I knew the way to ask questions without irritating him. I teased him, I soothed him, I hovered on the brink of going too far, and knew it delighted us both.

"Come and have tea with me," said Mrs. Fairfax, popping her head around the schoolroom door. I was glad to go downstairs, nearer, I imagined to Mr. Rochester's presence.

"It's a fine, starlit night, Mrs. Fairfax said. "Mr. Rochester has had a pleasant day for his journey."

"Journey?" I stuttered.

"Oh yes. He set off straight after breakfast. He's gone to Lord Ingram's place, quite a house party. He'll be gone for a week or more, I expect. All these fine, fashionable people… Lord Ingram's daughter, Blanche, was here once at a Christmas ball Mr. Rochester gave. She was the belle of the evening."

I was stunned into silence. Then I asked, "What was she like?"

"Tall, long graceful neck, olive skin, dark and clear, eyes rather like Mr. Rochester's, big and black. And such a fine head of hair, raven black done in a crown of braids, and in her white dress with a red flower in her hair, she looked a dream."

When I was alone, I spoke to myself angrily. I'd been wandering in imagination's boundless fields. I needed to return to the safe land of common sense.

Jane Eyre, you fool. You're only a governess. Mr. Rochester is a man of the world. You must be mad to love him. Take pen and paper, Jane Eyre. Draw your portrait. Call it: 'Portrait of a Governess, poor and plain'. Then draw Blanche Ingram, according to Mrs. Fairfax's description. Don't forget the raven ringlets. Or the long neck, the clothes, and the rose… call it: 'Blanche, a lady of rank'. Then who would Mr. Rochester prefer?

Thus I silenced myself.

A fortnight later, at breakfast, Mrs. Fairfax had a letter from him.

"Well, I sometimes think we are too quiet, but we'll certainly be active now," she announced.

I busied myself filling Adèle's mug with milk.

"He's coming in three days, he says, and bringing a lot of people with him. All the bedrooms must be prepared, the library and drawing room to be got ready, and I am to get more kitchen help. The ladies will bring their maids, and the gentlemen their valets, so we shall have a full house of it."

I thought all the rooms at Thornfield were clean enough, but I was mistaken. Three extra women came in to work. Such scrubbing, such brushing, washing of paint, beating of carpets, polishing of mirrors, such shining of silver, such airing of sheets, such lighting of fires, I'd never seen before. Adèle ran wild, jumping on mattresses and pillows piled up before the enormous fires that roared up the chimneys. I helped in the kitchens, learning how to make cheesecakes and French pastry.

Occasionally in all this topsy-turvydom, I saw Grace Poole. The door to the third floor was kept locked now, but once a day she came down to the kitchen to eat her lunch, just for one hour, and then she crept upstairs, tramping quietly in her slippers, back, no doubt, to some low-ceilinged chamber where she sat and sewed.

One of the new charwomen remarked of her:

"She gets good wages, I guess?"

"Yes," replied Leah. "I wish I had as good. But she understands what she has to do – it's not everyone who could do it, not even for all the money she gets."

Leah saw me. She gave her companion a nudge.

"Doesn't she know?" asked the charwoman.

Leah shook her head.

There was a mystery, then, at Thornfield Hall. A mystery which I was not intended to understand.

Finally, Mr. Rochester and his party of friends arrived. I watched their cavalcade from the schoolroom window upstairs. Two open carriages were filled with men and women. I could see them laughing amid fluttering veils and plumes. Before them, on his black horse, was Mr. Rochester, and riding by his side, a lady. Her purple riding clothes swept the ground, her veil streamed on the breeze, and gleaming through its folds shone raven ringlets. Blanche Ingram. I knew it was her.

I heard laughter, quick conversations, light,

tripping steps, and then closing of doors.

"They're changing into their best clothes for dinner," said Adèle, looking knowledgeable. "That's what happened when Maman had people to stay, in Paris. I wish I could be at dinner with them."

"Are you hungry, Adèle?"

"Yes! It's hours since I've eaten."

"I'll bring you some supper," I told her.

I slipped into the kitchen. I found a cold chicken, bread, a tart, knives and forks, and with this picnic, I went upstairs. Before I got there, all the bedroom doors seemed to open at once, and out poured a galaxy of fine people, in clothes gleaming in the last rays of sunset glowing through the windows. I hid myself at the end of the passage in a dark corner, staring at them. They left me with an impression of high-born elegance that I'd never experienced before.

I gave Adèle her supper, and took her to watch over the gallery into the hall below, drinking in the sounds. Someone was playing the piano, a lady was singing, chatter buzzed through the walls... but I found myself listening not to the music, but trying to single out, among the mingled tones, the voice of Mr. Rochester.

The next day, they set out to visit some place of interest, all in carriages, except for Mr. Rochester and Blanche Ingram, who rode side by side.

"He admires her," I said to Mrs. Fairfax. "And look how she leans her head towards him."

"You'll see her close up this evening," Mrs. Fairfax replied. "I told Mr. Rochester that Adèle wanted to meet his friends, and he said, "Let her come after dinner, and tell Miss Eyre to come too."

"I expect he was only being polite," I said.

"No, my dear. I said you might be shy, being unused to strangers, but he said, "Nonsense! Tell her she must come, that it is my particular wish."

I sighed, dreading the ordeal before me.

Adèle was in a state of ecstasy all day. She didn't sober down until she began to dress for the evening, but by the time she'd had her curls arranged, her pink silk frock put on, her sash tied, she was as grave as a judge. I changed into my best dress, and smoothed down my hair.

Adèle touched my knee.

"A rose, Miss Eyre, to complete my 'toilette'. Please?"

"You think too much about your 'toilette', Adèle," I replied, but I took a flower and fastened it in her sash. She gave a sigh of total happiness.

Down we went, into the drawing room. Eight ladies were present – the men were still in the dining room. They were like a flock of plumy birds, sinking onto sofas, all with glossy hair, all decked in jewels.

And Blanche! Yes, there she was, with her dark ringlets, but her eyes were fierce and hard – they reminded me of Mrs. Reed's – and her mouth was arched and haughty. She was talking about flowers to one of the other ladies, a Mrs. Dent, and I soon saw she was playing on Mrs. Dent's ignorance. It was clever, but not pleasant to see.

Adèle, chattering in English and French, flitted between the ladies. "What a love of a child!" they exclaimed, but Blanche sneered, "What a little puppet. Mr. Rochester's French ward, I suppose."

Coffee was served, and with it came the gentlemen. I sat in an alcove, half hidden by the curtains. I'd brought embroidery to occupy myself. I looked down at it, concentrating on my silk threads and silver beads, yet I saw him enter.

Why should he notice me? We were far apart.

Yet, from my hiding place, I could not stop looking at him. I found such pleasure in looking... a precious pleasure, pure gold, with a steely point of agony. His face, jet-black eyebrows, deep eyes, strong features, grim mouth were full of power that stole my feelings from me and joined them to him.

I had not meant to love him. I had tried to stop. But now, I found I loved him all over again. I told myself I must smother it. My love was not returned. Yet I knew also I could do no other than love him.

I saw Blanche Ingram take her coffee and stand by Mr. Rochester.

"What possessed you to take charge of such a little doll as that?" she asked, pointing to Adèle. "Where did you pick her up?"

"She was left on my hands," he replied.

"Couldn't you have sent her to school? I see you have a governess for her. Ugh! Governesses! I must have had about a dozen of them, half of them fools, the rest ridiculous." She laughed, curling her pretty, sneering mouth. "The whole tribe is a nuisance."

She sat down at the piano, spreading out her white robes, and played a prelude with brilliance, talking all the while. She seemed intent on exciting admiration and amazement.

"Now, sing for me, Mr. Rochester, and I will play for you."

Mr. Rochester sang. His voice was a strong baritone. Its force found a way through my ear to my heart, and as the last vibrations died away and the drawing room chatter resumed, I could take no more and slipped away.

My sandal had come undone. I knelt at the foot of the staircase to tie it, and I heard a door close, and footsteps. I rose, quickly.

I was face to face with Mr. Rochester.

Why didn't you speak to me?" he asked

I could have asked the same, but I replied, "I didn't want to disturb you, sir."

"You are pale. What is the matter?"

"Nothing, sir."

"Won't you return to the drawing room? You are leaving too early."

"I am tired, sir."

"And a little depressed."

"I am not," I began, but he interrupted.

"You are. I can see that tears are not far off. What does this mean? I'll find out another time, I swear, but so long as my visitors stay, I want you in the drawing room every evening. Good night, my..."

He stopped, bit his lip, and left.

Chapter 8

The Gypsy Speaks

The months of solitude when first I went to Thornfield had vanished. Noise and merriment took their place. The house had come alive. Its sad feelings seemed driven away.

Not mine. I was convinced that Mr. Rochester intended to marry Blanche Ingram. Her rank and connections surely gave her power and allure. I saw their exchanged glances, her curls near his cheek, their mutual whispering.

Reader, I loved him. I could not unlove him now – even if he did not notice me.

I wasn't jealous of Blanche. She wasn't worthy of jealousy. She was showy, but not genuine; well-educated, but not intelligent. She knew nothing of tenderness or goodness. She wasn't kind to Adèle. I often saw her push the little girl out of the way or order her from the room. I knew she didn't charm Mr. Rochester. If she had, I should have turned my face to the wall. If she had been a good woman, kind, genuine, deserving respect, then my heart would have been torn out.

I could think of nothing but Mr. Rochester and his future bride.

One night, three things happened. Mr. Rochester left suddenly, just before a visitor, a Mr. Mason called to see him, all the way from Jamaica, and a gypsy woman turned up at the door, demanding to tell fortunes.

"A gypsy! What is she like?" cried Blanche.

"A shockingly ugly creature," said Mrs. Fairfax. "She looks rough and dirty."

"A real sorceress," said Blanche. "Show her into

the library. I have a fancy to have my fortune told. We all would like it."

One by one, Mr. Rochester's friends went into the library and came out, shocked and giggling.

"She knows everything!" they cried, as if shattered that their secrets were no longer private, and in the tumult, a footman came up to me.

"Please, miss, the gypsy says there's one single young lady who's not yet had her fortune told. She insists that you come. Will you go?"

I nodded. I judged my secrets too unimportant to be guessed. I went into the library.

The gypsy sat hunched in a bonnet and shawl by the fire, her face almost hidden in the shadows.

"Well? Do you want your fortune told?" she demanded.

"You must please yourself. I warn you, I don't believe in it."

"I knew you were impertinent and independent. I heard it in your step," said the old woman. "Why don't you tremble?"

"I'm not cold."

"Why don't you turn pale?"

"I'm not sick."

"Why don't you show me your palm?"

"I'm not foolish."

"You are cold, you are sick and you are foolish."

"Prove it," I said.

"I will. You are cold because no one strikes the fire that is in you. You are sick because the best feelings given to you, you keep at bay. You are foolish because, even though you suffer, you will not take one step to meet them where they wait for you."

"That's easy to say of anyone who is a dependent, a governess, as I am."

"Wait! You are very near happiness. Kneel!"

I knelt, saying, "Don't keep me long, the fire scorches me."

She gazed at me, and began muttering. "The eye shines like dew. It looks soft and full of feeling. The mouth delights in laughter. It should speak much and smile often. The forehead declares, 'Reason holds the reins', whatever passions overtake her. Though strong wind, earthquakes and fire may sweep by, I shall follow her voice. Rise, Miss Eyre, the game is played out."

Was I dreaming? The gypsy's accent and gesture were as familiar to me as my own.

"Well, Jane, do you know me?" said Mr. Rochester, throwing off his shawl and bonnet.

"Well, sir, what a strange idea. You've been talking nonsense to try to make *me* talk nonsense, I think."

"Do you forgive me?"

"I'll try to, but it wasn't right. I think you should get back to your guests, and you have one extra visitor. Mr. Mason. He came when you were out."

The smile on Mr. Rochester's lips froze.

"Mason! Jamaica!" he said, repeating these syllables as in a dream, his face growing paler than ashes as he spoke. He sat down, holding my hand in both his own, gazing at me, troubled and low.

"My little friend," he said. "I wish I were on a quiet island with only you, with all danger and memory gone from me."

"Can I help you, sir?"

"I know you will, Jane. Where is Mason now?"

"Laughing and talking with all the others, sir."

"If all these people spat at me, what would you do, Jane?"

"Turn them out, sir," I said.

He sighed.

"Tell Mr. Mason to come in here, Jane, and then leave me."

It was late. After I had shown Mr. Mason into the library, I went to bed. As the clock struck midnight, I heard Mr. Rochester, cheerful and strong, saying, "Here's your room, Mason. Sleep well!"

I relaxed. Mr. Mason was no threat, after all. My mind at ease, I fell asleep.

Chapter 9

The Cry in the Night

I woke to hear a cry. Good God! What a cry.

The silent night was torn in two by a sharp, desperate sound from a room above my own. I heard a thud and a smothered voice – "Help! Help! Rochester, for heaven's sake, come!"

I flung on some clothes and shot into the passage. Doors all down the corridor were opening, gentlemen and ladies emerging, asking, "What is it?" "What's happened?" "Is it fire?" "Robbers?"

At the end of the passage, a door flung open, and Mr. Rochester appeared with a candle.

“It’s nothing. One of the servants had a nightmare, that’s all. Go back to bed, everyone.”

I knew this was a story to calm his guests. I went back, and waited for I knew not what. Stillness returned, until I heard a tap on my door, and the voice I expected to hear asked, “Are you up?”

“Yes, sir.”

“You don’t turn sick at the sight of blood?”

“I don’t think so.”

“Come with me, quietly. Bring a sponge, a cloth. You’re sure you don’t feel faint?”

He grasped my hand, and held it.

Up the stairs we went to the third floor. Mr. Rochester unlocked one of the doors, and led me inside a room I’d seen before, when Mrs. Fairfax first showed me over the house. It was hung with tapestry, but one of them was now looped up, revealing a till-now unseen door. A light shone from within, and I heard a snarling sound, like a dog, and then a shout of laughter. Grace Poole?

Mr. Rochester closed the door and locked it.

"Here, Jane," he said, and I saw a man sitting, his eyes closed, deathly white, his arm soaked in blood. It was the stranger, Mr. Mason.

"I'm done for," he groaned.

"Nonsense, only a scratch! Jane, I'll have to leave you here while I go for the doctor. Keep sponging the blood, and don't speak. Mason, don't you speak either. You'll agitate yourself, and make yourself ill."

He left the room. I heard the key in the lock. Here I was, fastened into a room on the third floor, a bleeding man before me, a murderess separated from me by a single door. I heard creaking steps, the snarling noise, and a deep human groan.

What crime was this, that lived here at Thornfield and could not be turned away? What mystery broke out, first in fire, and now in blood? Who was Mason?

I waited as minutes, half hours and hours ticked by, pressing the bloodied cloth to my patient, holding water to his lips, as he moaned and writhed. The candle eventually died out, but by now the first grey light of dawn was seeping through the edges of the curtains.

At last Mr. Rochester returned with Dr. Carter.

"I can give you just half an hour to bandage him up," he told the doctor, as he drew back the thick curtains to let in all the daylight he could.

"Is he fit to be moved?" asked the doctor, studying the wound. "How is this? The flesh is torn as well as cut. There have been teeth here."

"She bit me," murmured Mason. "I didn't expect it. She said she'd suck my blood, drain my heart..."

"I warned you," said Mr. Rochester. "Hurry. The sun will soon be up, and I must have him off."

Both half-carrying Mason, they took him downstairs. I followed.

The doctor's carriage disappeared down the driveway, as I watched by Mr. Rochester's side.

"A strange night, Jane," he said, leading me now to an arch in the wall, lined with ivy. "Were you afraid? You are pale."

"I'm afraid for you, sir. Your life is not safe,

while Grace Poole stays."

"Don't trouble yourself about her. As for my life, I can take care of myself. I stand, as always, on the edge of a volcano that vomits burning ash."

He paused. Sighed. And continued.

"Suppose, Jane, you were a wild boy who had made a terrible mistake. For twenty years you wandered in exile till you found the one who gave you everything you wanted. A gentle, gracious girl. Would you be justified in breaking the law for her?"

He looked at me. What was I to say? Was he talking of Blanche Ingram? The birds carolled their dawn chorus, and I was silent.

"Go through that shrubbery, Jane, back to the house. No one must see you here."

I heard him call out cheerfully, "Mason was even earlier than you! Gone before sunrise!"

He had espied some of his guests in the stables. He went one way, I another.

Blanche Ingram. Yes, he would marry her. He had as good as told me so.

Chapter 10

Lightning and Thunder Shake My World

The following afternoon, I had a visitor. Robert, the coachman from Gateshead Hall.

"The family is in a bad way, miss. Mr. John died a week ago. Very wild, he was. Got into debt and into jail. His mother helped him out a lot, but he ruined her. Missis is very ill now, and she cries out "Jane, Jane". So Miss Georgiana and Miss Eliza told me to find you and bring you to her."

"Of course I'll come," I said. I found Mr.

Rochester, and told him I was going to see a sick woman.

"Who is she?" he demanded. "What is she to you?"

"My aunt, sir."

"You told me you had no relations."

"She cast me off, sir. She disliked me."

"What good can you do her? I can't have you running off to see an old woman who cast you aside and may be dead before you get there."

"I must go," I said.

He grimaced. "Who will take you? The coachman? How long will you be gone?"

"Only a week, sir. But I must tell you that when you marry, I cannot remain here. You must send Adèle to school. I will advertise for another position."

"You will not," he growled. "Farewell for the present, Jane."

"Farewell, sir."

I reached Gateshead the following day. Bessie greeted me warmly. And then I went to my aunt.

She lay in bed with the same stern, stony eye, in the room I remembered so well. There I'd been whipped by her, ordered to kneel and ask pardon. I wanted now, more than anything, to forgive her, so I could be flooded with warm feelings.

She looked at me.

"Jane Eyre?"

"Yes."

"I had more trouble with that child than anyone would believe. Oh, she annoyed me, with her sudden bursts of temper. I wish she'd died, when so many children died at Lowood. I said she did."

What do you mean, aunt?"

"I'm very ill," she said. "I must ease my mind before I die. I have done you a great wrong." Shifting herself, she pointed to her dressing table.

"Open the drawer. Read the letter inside."

'*Dear Madam,*

Will you kindly give me Jane Eyre's address? I am her uncle, her father's brother. I wish to adopt her, and bring her to live with me in Madeira, where I have been blessed with making my fortune. I have no family, and intend to leave my wealth to her.

I am, Madam,

John Eyre, Madeira.'

It was dated three years back.

"Why did I never hear of this?" I asked.

"Because I hated you. I could not forget the way you spoke to me when you were a child. When you said the thought of me made you sick. Oh!" she groaned. "Water! Bring it quickly!"

"Dear Mrs. Reed," I said, offering her the drink. "Forgive the passionate words of a child. It was long ago."

"But I could not forget. I took my revenge. I didn't want to think of you happy and rich. I told your uncle you died of fever at Lowood. You were born to be my tormentor. My last hour is racked with guilt for a wrong which, but for you, I would never have done. You have a bad nature, Jane."

"I am not as bad as you think. Often, as a little child, I'd have been glad to love you if you would have let me. Can't you forgive? Kiss me, aunt."

I leaned over but, feeble as she was, she turned away, her glazed eyes avoiding my gaze.

"Love me or hate me as you will," I said at last, "you have my full forgiveness. Now, be at peace."

Poor, suffering woman. Dying, she would hate me still. So sad to die with a heart filled with hate.

I sat by her, but she was fast relapsing into unconsciousness. By midnight, she was dead.

I stood by her body with Eliza and Georgiana, gazing on it with pain. Her daughters did not speak, but neither of them shed a tear.

I stayed until she was buried, and then returned to Thornfield. I wanted to walk the last few miles through the fields, where the hay-making was nearly complete, between hedges full of roses. In the huge sky above me, the sun was setting, as warm as the feeling in me… I was going home.

No. I corrected myself. Thornfield could not be my home. Only for a few more weeks, until Mr. Rochester's marriage.

I climbed the stile into the garden, and saw Mr. Rochester, reading by the chestnut tree.

"Jane! Just like you to steal here in the twilight, not like any other mortal. Where have you come from?"

"I have been with my aunt, sir, who is dead."

"A truly Janian reply. She comes from the other world. Are you glad to be home?"

Despite my pride and intentions to show restraint, I said, "I am strangely glad to get back again to you. Wherever you are is my home."

I began to walk back to the house, but he caught me and held me fast.

"Turn back. On so lovely a night as this, it's a shame to be inside."

"You like Thornfield, don't you?" he asked. "And you're fond of Adèle too, and Mrs. Fairfax?"

"Yes, sir, in different ways, I love them both."

"You would be sorry to part with them?"

"Yes."

"It's always the way of the world," he said. "No sooner are you settled than you must move on."

"Must I move on, sir?"

"I think you must, Jane."

"Then you are going to be married, sir?"

"Exactly. With your usual acuteness, you have hit the nail on the head. In about a month, I hope."

"Then I must advertise, sir, for another situation."

"Another situation, eh? Really? How about Ireland? You'd like it. Such warm-hearted people in Ireland, they say."

"It's a long way off," I said. The very thought of it froze my heart. The ocean waves seemed to rush between me and the man by my side.

"The sea…" I murmured. "Such a barrier…"

"From what?"

"From England, and from Thornfield and…"

"Well?"

"From you, sir."

I did not mean to say this, nor did I welcome the tears that fell from my eyes.

"I love Thornfield," I said. "I love my life here.

I've been happy, and to go is like looking at death."

"Then don't go."

"I must, because of Miss Ingram – your bride."

"My bride? I have none."

"But you will…"

"Yes! I will! I will!" He set his teeth.

"I tell you, I must go!" I could take no more. Words poured from me. "Do you think I can stay to become nothing to you? Do you think I am a machine without feelings? Do you think because I am poor and plain that I have no heart? You think wrong – I have just as much soul as you. And if God had gifted me with beauty and wealth, I'd have made it as hard for you to leave me as it is now for me to leave you. As the world sees us we are not equal, but it is my spirit that speaks to your spirit, and we stand at God's feet – equal."

He enfolded me in his arms, pressing his lips on mine. "Jane, it is you I want. I want you as my wife."

I did not answer. I was incredulous.

"Do you doubt me, Jane?"

"Entirely."

"You thought I wanted to marry Miss Ingram? She – cold, fortune-hunting? No, Jane, poor and plain as you are, I beg you to accept me."

"Do you truly love me?"

"I do. I swear it."

"Then, sir, I will marry you."

"Call me Edward, my little wife."

"Dear Edward!"

"God forgive me," he said. "I will have her. I wash my hands of the world's judgement. I defy it."

We were in shadow. I could scarcely see my Edward's face. The wind roared and swept over us, making the chestnut tree writhe and groan. The rain rushed down, and we hurried back to the house, as he kissed me over and over again.

"We'll tell them all tomorrow," he said.

Early in the morning, Adèle came running in to tell me the chestnut tree had been struck by lightning in the night, and half of it split away.

Chapter 11

The Wedding Veil

Adèle was delighted by our news, but Mrs. Fairfax was astonished.

"Is it really true?" she asked me when we were alone. "I can scarcely believe it. He's so much older. He's rich, you're poor, and the Rochesters have always gone for money. Is it really for love?"

I was hurt. Tears rose in my eyes.

"Is it so impossible? Am I a monster?"

"No, my dear, you look much improved these days. But you're so young. You don't know anything about men. I fear something will be… not quite what you expect. I hope all will be right in the end."

"Never mind that now," I said impatiently, for Mr. Rochester was calling me.

He wanted to take me shopping. He took me to a silk warehouse where he wanted to buy me half a dozen silk dresses. I persuaded him to buy just two – the more he bought, the more my cheeks burned. I felt like a doll, being dressed by him and I hated it.

"Stop buying me things," I begged. "If you go on, I swear I'll be married in my old Lowood frocks. I don't want to be crushed by diamonds."

I decided to write to my uncle in Madeira, and tell him I was to be married. If he knew I was alive, and still wanted me as his heir, then I wouldn't be dependent on Mr. Rochester's impulsive generosity.

"We ought to get back for Adèle's lessons," I said.

"Enough of governess slavery," he retorted. "You're mine now."

"I won't stop," I said. "I'll earn my living until the end of time, and you shall give me nothing but..."

"But what?"

"But your love, and so we shall be equal."

He chuckled. "Who else would reject my gifts? Isn't it good to hear her? I wouldn't change this girl for anyone in the world!"

I smiled. My future husband was becoming the whole world to me. More than the world.

The month of our engagement passed quickly, until Mr. Rochester and I were having supper together the night before our wedding.

"This is the last time you will dine at Thornfield Hall for a long while," he said – but I could not eat. I pushed my plate away.

"Is it the thought of going away that takes away your appetite?" he asked.

"No, not that. I had a dream last night..."

"Tell me. You look so pale, so anxious. What do you fear? That I shall be a bad husband?"

"Never that. I know you love me. It's something very strange. I was looking at my wedding dress yesterday, and found beside it a box. I opened it and saw your present to me, a priceless lace wedding veil. And then I went to bed, and I dreamed. I dreamed that Thornfield Hall was a ruin, home only to bats and owls. I stumbled on a fallen piece of marble, the grass had grown through the door, and nothing but a shell-like wall remained. In the distance I heard a horse's hooves. I was sure it was you, that you were going far away. I ran after you, but the stones rolled beneath my feet, the ivy branches I was grasping gave way, and I lost my balance, fell, and woke."

"Only a dream, Jane."

"But there is more. When I woke, a yellow candlelight shone in my eyes, and I saw the cupboard door was open. I heard rustling. I sat up, and I saw a person I'd never seen before.

"Describe, Jane."

"A woman, tall and large, with thick dark hair hanging down her back, wearing a long white garment. She took my veil and put it on. She turned around – and then I saw her face. Oh! Her face! Big, savage, swollen lips, blood-shot angry eyes. She tore off my veil, ripped it in two and stamped on it. Then she shone her candle at me. I saw her face right over my own, and I fainted. Who was she? What was she?"

"She was nothing. Not real. The result of too much imagination."

"But she must have been real. In the morning, I saw the two halves of my veil – ruined."

Mr. Rochester started and shuddered.

"Thank goodness!" he exclaimed, pulling me close to him. "Only the veil was harmed. It was Grace Poole, Jane, and in your dream, you gave her the face of a fiend. Does that satisfy you?"

It did seem the only possible explanation.

"Don't sleep in your room tonight," he said. "Sleep with Adèle. Lock the door on the inside."

I never slept that night. I watched Adèle breathe in the innocent sleep of childhood. She seemed to be the symbol of my past life, the innocence I was leaving behind. I was ready for my unknown future.

Chapter 12

The Madwoman in the Attic

I dressed early the next day in my wedding gown. All was to be as simple as possible, just us and the clergyman. Mrs. Fairfax, Adèle and the servants waved at us as we walked to the church. We wanted no bridesmaids, no groomsmen, no relatives.

I glanced at Mr. Rochester and wondered if any bridegroom had ever looked so grimly resolute.

In the churchyard, I saw two strangers wandering among the tombstones. When they spied us, they went around the back of the church. I supposed they would slip in through the side door to witness the ceremony. Mr. Rochester didn't see them. He was looking at me, and together we entered the church.

The priest awaited us by the altar. The air was still. Only two shadows moved in a far-off corner.

The marriage service began. The priest explained the purpose of marriage and went on:

"...If either of you know of any reason why ye may not be lawfully joined together in holy matrimony, speak now..."

He paused, as is the custom. When is that pause ever broken by a reply? Then a voice cried out, "The marriage cannot go on. I declare an impediment."

The priest looked at the speaker who stepped from the shadows, but Mr. Rochester did not move.

"Proceed," he told the priest.

"Not till I know more," he replied. "What is the impediment?"

"Simply this," said the stranger. "Mr. Rochester already has a wife."

I looked at Mr. Rochester. His face was pale,

his eyes like flint. He clasped me to his side.

"Who are you?" he asked the stranger.

"My name is Briggs, a lawyer, from London."

"You would thrust a wife on me?"

"I can prove it." Mr. Briggs took a paper from his pocket and read out in a nasal, official voice,

"I, Richard Mason, affirm that Edward Rochester of Thornfield Hall was married to my sister, Bertha Mason, at Spanish Town, Jamaica. A copy of the marriage certificate is now in my possession."

"That may prove I was once married, but not that the woman is still living," said Mr. Rochester.

"She was three months ago," replied the lawyer. "I have a witness to that fact."

"Produce him, or get out," snapped Mr. Rochester.

The second shadow stepped forward.

Mr. Mason.

Mr. Rochester looked at him with contempt. Mason shook, white with nerves.

"She is living at Thornfield Hall," he bleated. "She's my sister. I saw her in April."

"Impossible," said the priest. "I've never heard of a Mrs. Rochester living there."

"No. I took care that none should hear of her. Come, everyone, leave the church. You must meet my wife. Bertha. She is mad. I married her fifteen years ago. I learned later that she came from a mad family, but I was cheated into marrying her. Yes, come and see Mrs. Poole's patient, my wife. This girl," he looked at me, "knew nothing. She never dreamed she was going to be dragged into a false union with a man who was already married."

Still holding my hand, he strode back to the house, followed by the gentlemen. Mrs. Fairfax, Adèle and the servants were waiting to greet us.

"No congratulations, please," he cried. "They are fifteen years too late. Come upstairs, everyone."

"You know this place, Mason, he said. "She bit and stabbed you here."

He opened the second door behind the tapestry.

I saw, by the fire, Grace Poole stirring a saucepan. In the shadows at the far end a figure ran back and forth. It was on all fours, growling like a wild animal. A mane of hair hid its face.

"How is she today, Mrs. Poole?" asked Mr. Rochester.

"Not too bad," she replied, but the creature, seeing him, stood up with a cry.

"Careful, sir," cried Grace Poole.

I recognized that face, those purple, bloated features… she sprang at Mr. Rochester. She squeezed his throat, and bared her teeth and laid them to his cheek. But he would not strike her. He wrestled, and finally got her into a chair.

"This," he said, "is my wife. And this is what I wished to have, this young girl who stands so quietly in her innocence. Compare her clear eyes with my wife's, this face with that mask, and then judge me. And now leave me with my prize."

The lawyer stopped me on the stairs.

"You are not to blame, madam. Your uncle will

be glad to hear it when Mr. Mason returns to Madeira."

"My uncle!" I exclaimed.

"Mr. Mason knows him. He was with him when your letter arrived, telling him of your intended marriage. He is a sick man, your uncle."

I hardly listened. I went straight to my bedroom and put on the plain gown of yesterday. I looked as I always did – yet who was I? Almost a bride, now a single girl again. A frost had killed her hopes.

I knew I must leave Mr. Rochester.

I opened my door. There stood Mr. Rochester right outside it.

"You've come out at last," he said. "I never meant to hurt you, Jane. Will you forgive me?"

I forgave him instantly. There was such sadness in his eyes. He bent to kiss me, but I turned away.

"Jane, I have another house, Ferndean Manor, even more rural and hidden than Thornfield. I could take you there now. I'll send Adèle to school, and we could live as man and wife. Grace can have charge of my wife anywhere, far away, to stop her from burning people in their beds at night, biting the flesh from their bones, stabbing them..."

"Sir, you speak of her with hate. Don't be cruel. She can't help being mad."

"Don't hate me, Jane. I love you. Let me tell you how it happened. My father and my elder brother said I must marry money. They sent me to Jamaica with an introduction to the rich Mason family. Before I knew it, I was engaged. I was dazzled, lied to, manipulated. They were desperate for their mad daughter to be wed. I'd never been alone with her, so I did not guess. My father and brother thought only of her thirty thousand pounds. They knew, as I did not, that lunacy ran through her entire family. I was in despair. I brought her back, to live here in the care of Grace Poole. Mrs. Fairfax had no idea, although she may have suspected something. Sometimes Grace has too much to drink and then Bertha escapes her guard."

"And you, sir? What did you do?"

"I travelled. I was lonely, miserable. I had nothing. And then I saw you, that frosty night. I leaned on you – do you remember? I knew my life had changed. You are my better self. Say you will stay with me. Say, "I will be yours."

"I cannot be your mistress, Mr. Rochester. We must both strive to do right."

"Jane!" he cried. "Won't you be my comforter? You are my life."

I heard my feelings speak in my heart. "Think of his misery! Save him, love him!"

Then again: "Don't give in to temptation."

"I am going, sir." I said. How hard it was to say these words.

"Oh Jane! My hope – my love – my life," broke from his lips.

I could not help it. I came back to kiss him, smoothing his hair with my hand.

"God bless you and keep you," I said, and this time, I had the strength to leave.

"Farewell," said my heart. "Forever."

Chapter 13
Alone

I left that day. I packed a small bundle of clothes and 20 shillings – all I had. I left behind everything Mr. Rochester had given me: clothes, jewels, money. They belonged to the bride who had melted away, not to me.

"Farewell, Mrs. Fairfax. Farewell, darling Adèle," I whispered as I crept downstairs. My hand moved to Mr. Rochester's door, but I pulled myself back.

Through the door… through the great gates… now I was out of Thornfield.

I crossed the fields, till I reached the road. A

coach passed. I hailed it and told the coach driver to take me as far as he could for 20 shillings. I sank back into the coach. What had I done? I'd cast myself into the wilderness. I was on my own. Reader, may you never feel what I suffered then, or weep such bitter tears.

Hours later, the driver set me down at a place called Whitcross, a crossroads in the middle of nowhere, with moorland all around. I realized that I'd left my bundle in the coach. I was now homeless, hungry, destitute. I had no money. I had nothing.

Where could I go? What could I do?

I wandered onto the moor, and found a sheltered place beneath a crag. I curled up under my shawl, with heather for my pillow. Exhausted, I slept.

The next day, I rose and followed the road. About two o'clock, I came to a village that boasted one shop, selling bread. I was faint with hunger.

"Would you give me just one roll?" I asked.

The shop woman stared at me suspiciously.

No, couldn't sell one roll on its own.

"Do you know anyone who might want a servant around here?"

She shook her head. So, on I went, through the village and out again to the wild empty moor. I passed a cottage where a small girl was about to throw a dish of cold porridge into the pig's trough.

"Will you give me that?" I asked.

"Mother," called the child. "A woman here wants this porridge."

"Well, lass, give it to her. The pig doesn't want it."

Ravenously, I devoured it, and walked on. Day turned into twilight, and with it, pitiless, drenching rain. I didn't see how I could sleep on the cold, wet ground. I was faint, chilled – I thought I would die.

Far off, I saw a light, flickering. It led me over a bog. I stumbled and I fell, but still I followed it. I came to a road, dark with fir trees. The light vanished. I put out my hands and felt the rough stones of a wall. I groped on. A whitish object gleamed before me – a gate. I'd come to a house.

Moor Cottage. I could just make out its name on the gate.

I wondered if its inmates were already in bed at this hour, but now, as I stepped onwards, its light shone so clearly that I could see through the window. A kitchen, brightly clean. A dresser with china plates, a clock, a scrubbed table, and an old woman knitting in a rocking chair by the fire. Two young women entered. I could hear them speak.

"You'll want some supper, to be sure," said the old woman. "It's late."

"Thank you, Hannah. I wonder when St. John will return."

Their faces were gentle and thoughtful. Listening, I gathered their names were Diana and Mary Rivers, that St. John was their brother and a clergyman, that Hannah was their servant.

I gathered myself together, one last effort, and knocked at the door. Hannah opened it a crack.

"What do you want?" she demanded.

"A night's shelter, in an outhouse, or anywhere,

and a morsel of bread."

"Get away! You shouldn't be wandering at this hour. Here's a penny. Now, be off."

"Don't shut the door!" I pleaded. "A penny cannot feed me. I've nowhere to go."

"I'll warrant you know well where to go, and if you're in league with burglars, you can tell them a gentleman lives here with a gun."

She closed the door.

"If I die, I believe in God." These words I said aloud. Death was near, I was certain.

"We must all die," said a voice behind me. "But I will not let you die here of want."

Who spoke? I could not see. I'd closed my eyes...

The door creaked open. Hannah again.

"St. John? Why, that woman's still there."

"You've done your duty, protecting us, Hannah," said St. John. "But I think this is an unusual case, and we should help."

Hearing the noise, Diana and Mary, came to the door.

"Poor thing, she does look pale."

"Thin, ill, like a ghost."

They took me to the kitchen fire, and fed me with bread dipped in milk. Little by little, I felt my senses return.

"Your name?" asked St. John.

"Jane Elliott." I had to avoid discovery.

"Where do you live? Where are your family, your friends?"

I was silent.

"What do you want us to do for you?" he asked.

"Forgive me. I cannot speak more," I said.

"We will leave you, and talk the matter over," said St. John. Presently, Hannah came back and helped me up the stairs, out of my wet clothes into clean nightwear and a warm bed. A glow of grateful joy flooded my exhaustion, and I slept.

For three days I stayed in bed. When Diana and Mary brought me food, I heard, between sleeping and waking, snatches of their conversation:

"Thank heavens she's here."

"Yes, she'd have been dead by morning if she'd stayed out all night."

"Who is she? Her clothes look good and she looks sensible, but not at all beautiful."

Never did I hear one word of regret that they'd taken me in. I was comforted.

On the fourth day, I got up, and Diana and Mary were out. I found Hannah in the kitchen. She gave me some potatoes to peel.

"Do you often go out begging?" she asked.

"I am no beggar," I replied.

"No – I think I see that. You sound like a lady. In fact, you look like a decent little thing. If I was mistaken in you, don't think too hard of me."

"I did think hard of you," I said. "You wanted to turn me out on a wild night. But I'll forgive you."

As we shook hands, St. John came in.

"Miss Elliott!"

I took no notice. I wasn't used to my new name. St. John raised his eyebrows.

"I am glad to see you better," he said. "Come into

my study. Perhaps now we can write to your friends and restore you to your home."

"Impossible," I said. "I have no home."

"No family? Unusual… Explain yourself."

"I am nineteen. I was an orphan, sent to Lowood School, where I was both pupil and teacher. Then I went out as a governess, where I was happy. I had to leave four days ago, through no fault of my own, and I ended up, here, with no money, destitute, after wandering for days and nights on the moor."

"Your name is not Jane Elliott?"

"No. It is the name I wish to be known by. I fear discovery above all things."

Diana and Mary came in now, their warmth a contrast to St. John's coldness.

"You shall stay here," they said.

"I'd like to work," I replied. "I don't want to be a burden. I'll do anything: be a servant, dressmaker."

"She must rest now," urged Diana. "She's still weak. Don't find her employment just yet, St. John."

Chapter 14

I Find My Family

The more I knew Diana and Mary, the more I liked them. They loved reading, they loved Moor Cottage, and the heath. The wild flowers, the breeze, the clear air, the distant crags gave them pleasure, as they did me. Our tastes were very alike.

St. John was more distant. He was often out, visiting the sick in his parish. I never heard him express love for the countryside. He seemed to be yearning for something that life did not give him.

After a month, I was fully recovered.

"I have heard of a job for you," St. John said.

"A schoolmistress is needed in a village school, a few miles away. You may not like it. It may not suit your accomplishments and intelligence. Your pupils are cottage children. Knitting, reading, writing, sums will be all they want to learn."

"Thank you, Mr. Rivers. I accept gladly."

"You can start next week. You'll have to live in a small cottage. No luxuries. It will be a simple, lonely life. You'll get thirty pounds a year."

"It's exactly what I want. I am not ambitious."

He gave a wry smile.

"Ambitious? Strange you should have chosen that word. If you are not ambitious, I think you are impassioned. By that, I mean that human affection means a lot to you. I think you will not be happy for long, alone."

I learned more then about St. John's character than in the whole month of our acquaintance.

St. John received a letter the day before I left.

"It's from the lawyer," he told his sisters. "Our Uncle John is dead. He's left his fortune not to us, but to another relation."

"We expected nothing," Mary said. "It would have relieved us of some poverty, but we are no worse off than we were before."

"Don't think us hard-hearted, Jane," said Diana. "We never knew this uncle. He quarrelled with our father. It was on his advice that our father lost all his money. We later heard he made a fortune of his own of twenty thousand pounds."

They didn't mention their lost fortune again, and the next day, I began my work.

My new home was a little two-roomed cottage. Downstairs, was a room with a sanded floor, a table, a chair. Upstairs, my bedroom held a narrow bed and a chest of drawers. I felt lost, as if I'd taken a step down, not up. I could have been with Mr. Rochester, in some sunny, foreign villa. He did love me, but I knew it was better to be an honest schoolmistress than in a fool's paradise of pretence and shame. Five weeks ago, I was an outcast. Now I could hold my head up high. I was independent.

My pupils at first seemed hopeless. Again, my first impressions were wrong. I found, as I taught them, that they were polite and eager to learn. I taught them about literature, history and geography, as well as basic arithmetic and spelling. I came to know their parents too. They invited me into their homes where I spent many happy hours.

Sometimes, St. John came to see how I was getting on. He told me one day that he'd decided to become a missionary, to leave home and preach God's word in India. He said this in his usual voice of measured steadiness, quiet, yet determined.

I was drawing when he came. Sheets of paper lay on my table. I put down my pencil to listen.

"I want to rise in the world," he told me. "Reason, not feeling, is my guide. I admire talent, endurance, hard work. You have these qualities. You are energetic. You are orderly."

He was beside me, looking at my drawings. Suddenly he picked up a torn off piece of paper, inspected it, and put it in his pocket.

His lips parted. He seemed about to speak.

"What's the matter?" I asked.

"Nothing," he replied. "Good afternoon, Miss Elliott." And he vanished.

I carried on drawing. I couldn't solve the mystery.

When St. John left, it was beginning to snow. The whirling storm went on all night. Next day, the weather was worse. A high wind brought blinding falls and drifts of snow. I had to put a mat against my door to stop it from blowing in. I lit a candle, and began to read a book of poetry.

I heard a noise – the wind, I supposed, but it was St. John opening the door latch, appearing like an icicle out of the howling darkness.

Why had he come, in this snowstorm?

"Has there been bad news?" I asked, startled.

"No. How easily alarmed you are." He stamped the snow from his feet. "I had hard work to get here. The snow was up to my waist."

"But why are you here?"

"To talk with you."

He stood there, his face handsome as chiselled marble, equally cold, though the firelight shone on him. Puzzled, I was silent.

He continued, "Or perhaps – not talk, but I want to tell you a story. I will begin. Twenty years ago a poor man fell in love with a rich man's daughter and married her. Her family disowned her, and two years later, both of them were dead, leaving behind a baby girl. She was taken to her rich relations, and brought up by her aunt, Mrs. Reed of Gateshead. You look startled. Did you hear a noise? I expect it was only a rat. Plenty of rats in these old cottages. Listen further. Mrs. Reed kept the orphan for ten years and then sent her to Lowood School, where she was a pupil and a teacher, like you. The facts are very like your story, aren't they? Then she left Lowood and became a governess to Mr. Rochester's ward."

I began to speak, but he interrupted.

"I've nearly finished. Hear me to the end. Mr. Rochester proposed marriage to the girl, but at the altar she discovered he already had a wife, a lunatic. She left that night, and no one knew where she went, though it has become a matter of urgency that she is found. Advertisements have been put in the paper. I have had a letter about her from a lawyer, Mr. Briggs. A strange story, don't you think?"

"Tell me this," I begged. "Since you know so much. How is Mr. Rochester?"

"I have no idea. Mr. Briggs' letter did not say. Shouldn't you be asking me the name of the governess?"

"But didn't Mr. Briggs write to him?"

"Of course. The letter was answered by a Mrs. Fairfax."

My poor master. He must have gone abroad. Gone – left England. My worst fears were realized.

"He must have been a bad man," said St. John.

"You don't know him – don't judge him."

"Very well. I'm more interested in finishing my tale about the governess. Don't you want to know her name? Here it is."

He put before me a torn-off piece of paper. It was the scrap he'd picked up the previous night, when I'd been drawing at the table. I'd scribbled, in an absent-minded moment, my own name: Jane Eyre.

"Briggs wrote to me of a Jane Eyre. I knew a Jane Elliott. Shouldn't you ask why Briggs wanted to know about you?"

"Well, what did he want to know?"

"To tell you your uncle was dead, that he has left you all his property, and now you are rich."

"I! Rich?"

"Very rich indeed. Twenty thousand pounds."

To say I was amazed could not describe what I felt. I was independent, at last. Of course I was pleased, but I was also sorry. I had wanted to see my uncle, the last member of my family.

"You must prove your identity, of course," said St. John, "but that shouldn't be difficult. Well, Miss Eyre, I must go through the snow again, now I have told you your news. Good night."

"Stop!" I cried. "Why did Mr. Briggs write to you?"

"I am a clergyman, and clergy are often asked this sort of thing."

"That doesn't satisfy me. Tell me more."

"I suppose you must know some time. My mother's name was Eyre. She had two brothers. One went to Madeira. The other, your father, married a Miss Reed of Gateshead. Our Madeira uncle left all his money to his orphan niece, Jane Eyre."

"Wait!" I said. That means we are cousins – you, me, Diana and Mary." I was smiling, laughing, clapping my hands with joy.

"You seem more excited by that than by the fact you are an heiress," said St. John.

"Don't you see?" I exclaimed. "I am no longer alone! I have a family. I have cousins. We'll share the legacy. I don't need all that money for myself. We are a family. Diana and Mary are like my sisters, and you – my brother."

Chapter 15

Choosing...

I gave up my job at the school and came back to Moor Cottage. I was sorry to say goodbye to my pupils. I'd grown very fond of them, and I felt they liked me. They'd been presented to me as backward cottage children with low expectations, but I'd found them intelligent, curious and rewarding.

"Aren't you pleased you've done some real good with them?" asked St. John. "Wouldn't you like to go on teaching?"

"Yes. I'm pleased, but I need time away," I said. "I am content. Let me, for now, be useful here."

I kept my word. I went on a spending spree with my newly inherited money, buying new furniture, carpets and pretty things for Moor Cottage, turning it into a bright, snug home. Diana and Mary were delighted, but I don't think St. John noticed. He was absorbed in learning Hindustani.

One afternoon, Diana and Mary went out, leaving me alone in the sitting room with St. John. I could feel his ice-blue gaze, watching me.

Unexpectedly, he said, "Jane, I want you to learn Hindustani. It will help me to have a pupil. It will fix words and grammar in my mind more readily. It won't be for long. I leave for India in three months."

I agreed to help. It was hard to refuse. But life had been easier when he'd taken no notice of me. He was patient but demanding. I felt him watching me all the time. I found I could no longer talk and laugh freely. I wanted to do well, and to please him, but it seemed to me that, in doing so, I was untrue to my nature. I found I was forcing myself to fit into his ideas. I fell under his freezing spell.

Once, at bedtime, his sisters and I stood around him, saying goodnight. He kissed each of them.

"St. John, Jane is your third sister now," said Diana. She was in a playful mood. "Kiss her too." She pushed me towards him. St. John bent his head and kissed my cheek, his eyes questioning mine. There are no such things as ice kisses, or I should say his kiss was made of ice. I felt it had sealed something in his mind, for he always kissed me goodnight afterwards.

The Hindustani lessons progressed, as spring grew into summer. The changing seasons brought me no happiness. Mr. Rochester was always in my thoughts. What had happened to him? Was he ill? I had to know. I wrote to Mrs. Fairfax, but received no reply. My spirits sank. More and more, I felt my life was on hold, stilled, without hope.

One day, as I sat with St. John, trying to read an Indian manuscript, my voice broke. My words were lost in sobs.

"Come outside," he said. "We'll go for a walk."

Ten minutes later, we were on the moor. It was beautiful, spangled underfoot with star-like yellow flowers. A breeze came over the hills. The river, swollen by spring rains, rushed by with blue and golden gleams.

"In six weeks, I shall be gone," St. John said. "Jane, come with me to India, to take God's word to the people there."

"What?" I cried.

"God meant you to be a missionary's wife," he continued. "I claim you, not for myself, but for God. I've watched you. You work well, and have a sense of duty. You would be a help to me."

I knew I could do the work he wanted me to do, but my heart would not be in it. But if I stayed here, what then? England without Mr. Rochester was an empty land. St. John would never love me. But if I went to India, I could at least work, and forget. But not as his wife.

"I will go, but as your sister. I can't marry you."

"Impossible. We must be married. You must

see that. How can I, a clergyman, take with me to India a girl of nineteen?"

"I can't," I repeated.

"You have a man's brain, but a woman's heart. It would not work, Jane. You are not my sister."

"I have a woman's heart," I agreed, "but not for you. For you, I have only friendship."

"We must be married," he said. "In time, I expect, love would follow."

"I scorn your idea of love," I cried. "I scorn you for what you offer."

"I've done nothing to deserve your scorn," he replied, in anger or surprise, I couldn't tell.

"Perhaps not, but our ideas about love are too different. Dear cousin, forget all ideas of marriage. It would kill me. You are killing me now."

"Violent, unfeminine words, Jane, but I forgive you." His voice was gentle now, and he drew me to him. "Could you not consider it?"

Oh, that gentleness! Far more powerful than force. I almost melted in this gentleness. If only I knew for certain what was right. How was I to know? I prayed: Show me! Show me the path.

My heart beat fast. Suddenly it seemed as if an electric shock passed through it.

"What have you heard? What do you see?" St. John asked.

I saw nothing, but heard a voice somewhere cry, "Jane! Jane! Jane!"

"What is it?" I gasped.

It came, not from the air, nor from the earth, but I heard it. A human voice, well remembered, and loved. The voice of Edward Rochester. It spoke in pain, wildly and urgently.

"I am coming!" I cried. "Wait for me! Oh, I will come! Where are you?"

"Where are you?" I ran away from St. John, as the hills sent the echo faintly back. Where are you?

There was no answer. The wind sighed low in the trees. Silence and loneliness brooded over the moor.

Chapter 16

The Fire

I rose at dawn the following day and packed my clothes. I saw a note under my door:

You left me too suddenly yesterday. Take care that you do not make the wrong decision. Yours, St. John.

He wasn't at breakfast. I announced to Diana and Mary that I was going on a journey.

"Alone, Jane?" they asked. "Today?"

"Yes. I want to discover what's happened to a friend, who I've been worried about for some time."

I walked to the crossroads at Whitcross, where I caught the coach. It was the same vehicle that had brought me here from Thornfield. Now I was going back there. I had to know how Mr. Rochester was.

My excitement grew as the countryside became more and more familiar.

"How far is Thornfield Hall from here?" I asked the coachman.

"Two miles, down the fields."

I paid my fare, gathered my things and jumped down. I ran through the fields, recognizing every tree, hedge and stile. I felt I loved each one... I was coming home!

I stopped by a pillar. A pair of them, with stone balls on top, stood by a meadow gate. I was storing up my joy. My first view would be the front, where the battlements rose proudly against the sky.

The rooks cawed overhead. Perhaps they were watching me. I looked towards a lovely house. I saw a blackened ruin. The front was as I'd once seen it in a dream. A shell-like wall, fragile, no roof, no battlements, no chimneys – all had crashed in.

There was the silence of death about it. Weeds

had sprung up between the fallen walls and hollow windows. Empty, desolate, charred. Fire. But what story lay behind it? Had people died? If so, who?

Oh, where was Mr. Rochester?

I had to have answers. I raced to the nearest inn, and questioned the innkeeper, a pleasant-looking middle-aged man. I hardly knew how to begin.

"You know Thornfield Hall," I managed to say.

"Yes, ma'am. I lived there once. I was the late Mr. Rochester's butler."

"The late Mr. Rochester!" I gasped. "Is he dead?"

"I mean, old Mr. Rochester. Mr. Edward's father."

I breathed again. Since he was not in the grave, I could bear anything now.

"Is Mr. Rochester at Thornfield now?" I asked, knowing the answer, but I needed to slow down.

"No, ma'am. You must be a stranger to these parts, or you'd have heard what happened. Thornfield Hall is a ruin. It was burned down. Everything was destroyed. The fire broke out at dead of night. A terrible sight. I saw it myself."

At dead of night. Yes, that was the hour she always struck.

"How did the fire start?" I asked.

His voice dropped to a confidential hush.

"Did you ever hear of a lady – a lunatic – kept in the house?"

"I heard something about it."

"No one ever saw her. There was gossip… but she turned out to be his wife! There was a young lady, a governess, that Mr. Rochester fell in love with..."

I dreaded hearing my own story.

"The fire," I said urgently. "Tell me about it."

"I'm coming to that. The servants said they'd never known a man so in love. She wasn't at all beautiful – a little, small thing, not yet twenty, and he was twice her age. And he wanted to marry her."

"Did the mad woman start the fire?"

"You've hit the nail on the head. She was cared for by Mrs. Poole, a trustworthy nurse, but too fond of gin. Very understandable, for she led a grim life.

When Mrs. Poole was asleep, the mad lady would escape. They say she once set fire to her husband in his bed. On this night, she set fire to the governess's bed, but luckily there was no one in it. The governess had run away. Mr. Rochester searched for her as if she was the most precious thing on earth but not a trace of her could be found. After that, Mr. Rochester changed. He insisted on being alone. He sent his housekeeper away, and the little girl to school. He was like a hermit, shut up at the Hall."

"Then he didn't go abroad?"

"No. He wouldn't leave the house, except to wander in the grounds at night, like a ghost."

"Then he was at home when the fire started?"

"Yes, and he got the servants out of their beds and helped them out, and then he went back into the flames to rescue his wife. There she was, standing on the roof – I saw her with my own eyes – waving her arms above the battlements. A big woman, with long black hair, streaming against the flames. Mr. Rochester climbed though the skylight.

But as he got close, she yelled, and sprang, and next minute, she lay smashed on the ground."

"Dead?"

"Dead as the stones spattered with her blood."

"Good heavens."

"It was dreadful, ma'am."

"And Mr. Rochester?"

"Better if he'd died too. He's stone blind. Some say it was a judgement on him, but I pity him. As he was coming downstairs, a beam fell on him. One eye was knocked out, the other inflamed, and his hand was so crushed, the surgeon had to amputate. He's helpless. Blind and a cripple."

"Where is he?"

"At Ferndean, about thirty miles off. A wild, lonely place. He has his servant, John, to help him."

"Have you got any sort of cart or carriage?"

"A pony cart, ma'am."

"Take me to Ferndean, now, and I'll pay you twice the sum you'd normally charge."

Chapter 17

I Find My Love

I arrived at dusk. He was standing on the doorstep, his hand stretched out, as if feeling whether it rained. His hair was still raven black, his figure as tall, but he seemed desperate and brooding. Then he went inside, one hand feeling the way, the other, the mutilated one, tucked inside his coat.

I followed him. I found the kitchen, where John was preparing a tray with some water and candles.

John stared at me as if he'd seen a ghost.

"Is it really you, Miss Eyre?"

"Yes, John. Are the candles for Mr. Rochester?"

"He always wants candles at this hour, even though he's blind."

"Give the tray to me. I'll take them to him."

In the sitting room, Mr. Rochester's old dog, Pilot, lay curled on the floor, but jumped up when I came in. With a yelp, he bounded at me.

"What is the matter?" asked Mr. Rochester.

"Down, Pilot," I said.

"Is that you, John?"

"John is in the kitchen. Will you have some water?"

"Who speaks? What speaks?"

"John knows me. Pilot knows me."

"Good heavens! Am I mad? What sweet madness has seized me? Oh, I cannot see, but I must feel…"

"No madness, sir."

He groped. I held his hand with my own.

"Her fingers!" he cried. "Her small fingers, her neck, her waist… it is Jane!"

"I am here," I said. "I have come back to you."

"Not a dream?" he asked. "I dream of you and

wake, and find it was all a sham. Kiss me before you disappear, sweet dream…"

I pressed my lips to his.

"I'm real. I will not leave you, ever again, as long as I live. I will be your nurse, whatever you like."

"But not forever, Jane. One day you will marry."

"I don't care about being married. I am an independent lady. My uncle in Madeira died, and left me his fortune."

"Rich? If I were not such a blind wreck, I'd make you care. Where have you been, these past weeks?"

"With my cousins. St. John Rivers, and his sisters."

"Was he handsome, this St. John Rivers?"

"Very, sir."

"Did he want to marry you?"

"He did, sir. But I did not want to marry him."

"Jane, will you marry me?"

"Yes."

"Though I'm blind and crippled? No better than the old lightning-struck tree at Thornfield?"

"You are no lightning-struck tree. New plants will grow among your roots. To be your wife is the only thing I want upon this earth."

"Truly, Jane?"

"Most truly."

"Oh my darling! We have nothing in this world to wait for. We must be married instantly."

He looked and spoke eagerly. His old impetuosity was coming back. We talked, then. He told me how, in his loneliness, he had begun to pray for forgiveness. He thought I was dead. At last he felt so desolate, so tormented, that he could not take any more. He cried aloud the words: "Jane! Jane! Jane!"

"When?" I asked. "Was it last Monday?"

"It was. And – you will think I'm superstitious – but I thought I heard your voice. You called, "I am coming. Wait for me. Where are you?"

I pondered these things in my heart. I said nothing. But I thought, if there is a God, that he had heard, and answered, and forgiven.

Chapter 18

The End of the Story

Reader, I married him. I feel so blessed. Our love is so strong, beyond words. No woman was ever nearer her husband than I am.

As soon as I could, I went to see Adèle at her school. I found her pale and unhappy, frantic with joy at seeing me again. I took her home where she has been ever since. She is a good and loving girl.

Mr. Rochester continued blind for two years, and perhaps it was this that drew us even closer to each other, for I was literally his vision. But one morning at the end of two years, he asked, "Jane, have you a glittering chain around your neck?"

I answered, "Yes."

"And a pale blue dress?"

I had.

Eventually he recovered the sight of that eye. He cannot see the world as clearly as he did before, but the sky is no longer a blank to him. When his first-born child was put in his arms, he could see that the boy had inherited his own eyes as they once were – large, brilliant and black.

My Edward and I have been married for ten years. We are happy, the more so because all who we love are happy too. Diana and Mary are married. St. John, in India, is full of courage and devotion in his work. In his last letter, he told me he was ill, and that the end was near. I know that the next letter from India will be from a stranger, telling me he is no more. Brave St. John. He has lived the life he wanted. His hope was sure, his faith unclouded.